We Read
PHONICS™

Who Took the Cookbook?

TREASURE BAY

Parent's Introduction

Welcome to **We Read Phonics**! This series is designed to help you assist your child in reading. Each book includes a story, as well as some simple word games to play with your child. The games focus on the phonics skills and sight words your child will use in reading the story.

Here are some recommendations for using this book with your child:

1 Word Play

There are word games both before and after the story. Make these games fun and playful. If your child becomes bored or frustrated, play a different game or take a break.

> I can make the word clown!

CL OW N
F OO D

Many of the games require printed materials (for example, sight word cards). You can print free game materials from your computer by going online to www.WeReadPhonics.com and clicking on the Game Materials link for this title. However, game materials can also be easily made with paper and a marker—and making them with your child can be a great learning activity.

2 Read the Story

After some word play, read the story aloud to your child—or read the story together, by reading aloud at the same time or by taking turns. As you and your child read, move your finger under the words.

Next, have your child read the entire story to you while you follow along with your finger under the words. If there is some difficulty with a word, either help your child to sound it out or wait about five seconds and then say the word.

3 Discuss and Read Again

After reading the story, talk about it with your child. Ask questions like, "What happened in the story?" and "What was the best part?" It will be helpful for your child to read this story to you several times. Another great way for your child to practice is by reading the book to a younger sibling, a pet, or even a stuffed animal!

So what did you like most in this book?

I liked that the ending was a big surprise!

LEVEL 7   **Level 7** introduces words with vowel combinations "ou" and "ow" (as in *out* and *owl*), "oi" and "oy" (as in *oil* and *boy*), "aw" (as in *hawk*), "oo" (as in *book*), and "oo" (as in *cool*).

Who Took the Cookbook?

A We Read Phonics™ Book
Level 7

Text Copyright © 2012 Treasure Bay, Inc.
Illustrations Copyright © 2012 Kelly Light

Reading Consultants: Bruce Johnson, M.Ed., and Dorothy Taguchi, Ph.D.

We Read Phonics™ is a trademark of Treasure Bay, Inc.

Published by
Treasure Bay, Inc.
P.O. Box 119
Novato, CA 94948 USA

Printed in Malaysia

Library of Congress Catalog Card Number: 2011942418

Hardcover ISBN: 978-1-60115-347-0
Paperback ISBN: 978-1-60115-348-7
PDF E-Book ISBN: 978-1-60115-594-8

We Read Phonics™
Patent Pending

Visit us online at:
www.TreasureBayBooks.com

PR-6-12

Who Took the Cookbook?

By Paul Orshoski

Illustrated by Kelly Light

Phonics Game

Alphabet Soup

Creating words using certain letter combinations will help your child read this story.

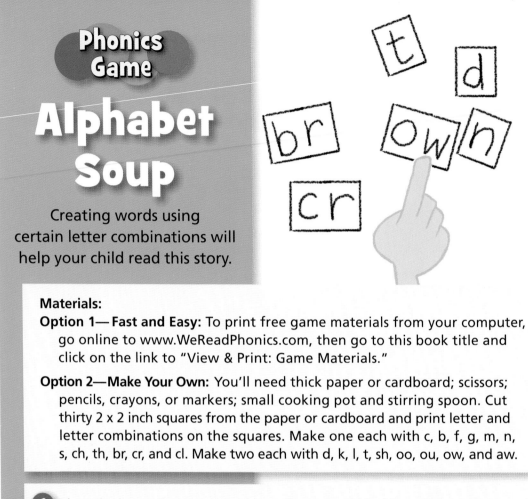

Materials:

Option 1—Fast and Easy: To print free game materials from your computer, go online to www.WeReadPhonics.com, then go to this book title and click on the link to "View & Print: Game Materials."

Option 2—Make Your Own: You'll need thick paper or cardboard; scissors; pencils, crayons, or markers; small cooking pot and stirring spoon. Cut thirty 2 x 2 inch squares from the paper or cardboard and print letter and letter combinations on the squares. Make one each with c, b, f, g, m, n, s, ch, th, br, cr, and cl. Make two each with d, k, l, t, sh, oo, ou, ow, and aw.

1. Place the letters into a pretend pot of soup and stir the pot! Then players take turns taking letters from the pot. When a player can make a word by putting his letters together, he makes and reads the word out loud. Once a word is made, the player can use the letters in that word (and other letters) to make new words. If scoring, give a point for each word that is made.

2. Players take turns taking letters and making words. Once a player has nine letters, he must put one letter back in the pot in order to take another letter.

3. If scoring, the word *cookbook* can be a bonus word worth an extra point. If a player can make *cookbook* and *chow* at the same time, he automatically wins!

4. The winner is the first player to score 12 points. Then, put all the letters back into the pretend pot of soup and play again!

Some words that can be made with these letters include *look, cookbook, good, food, shook, crook, crowd, brown, clown, chow, shout, mouth,* and *saw.*

Sight Word Game

Memory

Give!

OK, now pick another card.

GIVE

This is a fun way to practice recognizing some sight words used in the story.

Materials:

Option 1—Fast and Easy: To print free game materials from your computer, go online to www.WeReadPhonics.com, then go to this book title and click on the link to "View & Print: Game Materials."

Option 2—Make Your Own: You'll need 18 index cards and a marker. Write each word listed on the right on two cards. You will now have two sets of cards.

1 Using one set of cards, ask your child to repeat each word after you. Shuffle both decks of cards together, and place them face down in a grid pattern.

2 The first player turns over one card and says the word, then turns over a second card and says the word. If the cards match, the player takes those cards and continues to play. If they don't match, both cards are turned over, and it's the next player's turn.

3 Keep the cards. You can make more cards with other **We Read Phonics** books and combine the cards for even bigger games!

could

would

together

again

give

know

once

round

thanks

The cook in our lunchroom
makes really good chow.
The food that she makes
has us all shouting "Wow!"

Her treats are outstanding.
Her beets make us proud.
She broils up chicken
        that draws a big crowd.

She simmers up cheese
that we like on our chips.
Her hot toasted cookies
give joy to our lips.

We love the sweet taffy
she made yesterday.
If food got a grade, hers
would get a big "A"!

However, today
it is awful and foul!
The mouthful I took I
spit out in a towel.

The salad was droopy.
The green beans were brown.
We all hollered "Yuck!" and
that made the cook frown.

The eggs were not boiled.
The sausage was raw.
It was really disgusting—
the things that we saw!

One student was pouting.
She started to wail.
"I may just throw up! Would
you grab me a pail?"

The cook was upset, and
she started to cry.
"My food is no good,
and you need to know why."

"My cookbook is missing!
There must be a crook!
I left it right here
on this chair in my nook!"

"My cookbook explains
all the things I must do.
Without it my meals will
be too hard to chew."

"My food is now bad when it
once made you drool.
We must find that cookbook!
Please scan the whole school."

So who took the cookbook?
A prowler? A goon?
We had to find out,
    and we had to know soon.

Our class clown was cornered.

He said, "Why blame me?

I do not like books."

So we let him go free.

We hunted for hours.

We peeked 'round and 'round.

The cookbook, it seemed, was

just not to be found.

We sent for a hound dog.

Would he bring us luck?

He stepped in some taffy.

His paws were soon stuck.

The dog could not move,
 so I helped pull him free.
And then I found out
 he was sticking to me.

Some boys said, "No problem!
We know what to do."
And soon we were ALL
stuck together like glue!

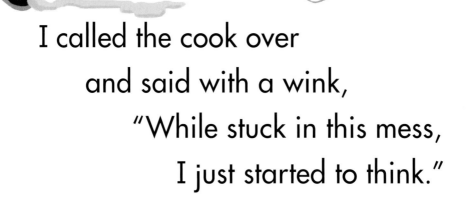

I called the cook over
and said with a wink,
"While stuck in this mess,
I just started to think."

"Would you turn around?
Let me have a good look."

THE BEST
COOK
BOOK
E V E R !

There, stuck to her dress
was the missing cookbook!

er face filled with joy.

   She said "thanks" with a grin.

      "I vow I will NEVER cook taffy again!"

Phonics Game

Word Search

Rereading words from the story will help your child become more comfortable reading those words.

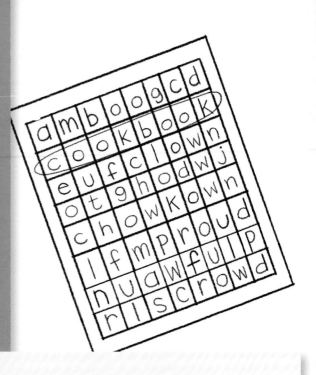

Materials:

Option 1—Fast and Easy: To print free game materials from your computer, go online to www.WeReadPhonics.com, then go to this book title and click on the link to "View & Print: Game Materials."

Option 2—Make Your Own: You'll need graph paper or a sheet of paper; marker and/or pencil; and ruler. Use the graph paper or make a grid on a sheet of paper that is 8 squares across and 8 squares down. Write these letters on the first line, one letter per square: a, m, b, o, o, g, c, d.

Write these letters on the second line, one letter per square:
c, o, o, k, b, o, o, k

Continue writing these letters on subsequent lines:
e, u, f, c, l, o, w, n
o, t, g, h, o, d, w, j
c, h, o, w, k, o, w, n
l, f, m, p, r, o, u, d
n, u, a, w, f, u, l, p
r, l, s, c, r, o, w, d

 Try to find these words in the word search. Words can be across or down. Circle the words when you find them.
mouthful, cookbook, clown, good, proud, chow, awful, crowd

Make a Face

Help your child practice some of the words in the story.

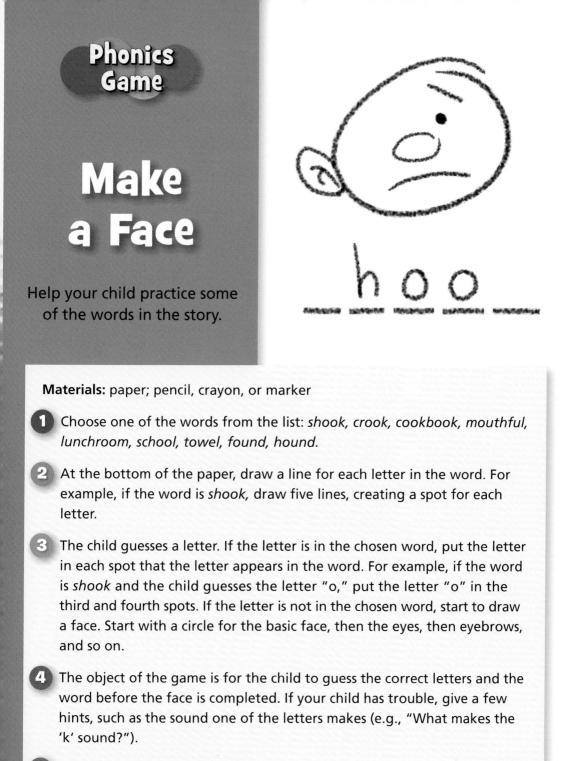

Materials: paper; pencil, crayon, or marker

1. Choose one of the words from the list: *shook, crook, cookbook, mouthful, lunchroom, school, towel, found, hound.*

2. At the bottom of the paper, draw a line for each letter in the word. For example, if the word is *shook,* draw five lines, creating a spot for each letter.

3. The child guesses a letter. If the letter is in the chosen word, put the letter in each spot that the letter appears in the word. For example, if the word is *shook* and the child guesses the letter "o," put the letter "o" in the third and fourth spots. If the letter is not in the chosen word, start to draw a face. Start with a circle for the basic face, then the eyes, then eyebrows, and so on.

4. The object of the game is for the child to guess the correct letters and the word before the face is completed. If your child has trouble, give a few hints, such as the sound one of the letters makes (e.g., "What makes the 'k' sound?").

5. Play again with another word.

If you liked *Who Took the Cookbook?*,
here is another **We Read Phonics** book you are sure to enjoy!

I Want to Be a Cowboy

Roy has a cowboy hat. He has cowboy boots. Now Roy wants to be a real cowboy! He goes to a dude ranch, where he can do lots of cowboy things. But at the ranch, Roy finds out that being a real cowboy is much harder than he expected.